Fire *in the* Valley

by Tracey West

SILVER MOON PRESS

FIRE IN THE VALLEY
by Tracey West

Copyright © by Kaleidoscope Press, Inc.

First Silver Moon Press Edition 1993

For information:
Silver Moon Press
New York, NY
(800) 874-3320

Design: John J. H. Kim
Cover Illustration: Nan Golub

Library of Congress Cataloging-in-Publication Data

West, Tracey, 1965-
    Fire in the valley / by Tracey West. -- 1st ed.
    p. cm. -- (Stories of the States)
    Summary: Twelve-year-old Sarah's feelings about life on
her family's California farm change when she writes a letter to
President Teddy Roosevelt to protest diverting water for use by the
growing city of Los Angeles and when she saves her twin brother
from a fire.
    ISBN 1-881889-32-7 : $14.95
    [1. Farm life--California--Fiction. 2. California--Fiction.
3. Brothers and sisters--Fiction..] I. Title. II. Series.
PZ7.W51937Fi 1993
[Fic]--dc20   93-22571
                                                         CIP

10 9 8 7 6 5 4 3 2
Printed in the USA

STORIES OF THE STATES

TABLE OF CONTENTS

CHAPTER ONE
Washing Hogs Is Woman's Work

"Sarah Jefferson, you get off that horse right now or I'm telling Pa!" Samuel Jefferson called. Sarah dug her heels into the horse's flanks.

"Giddyap, Rusty," she said, ignoring her brother.

The horse broke into a gallop, and Sarah's heart raced as the ground below her became a blur. The towering Sierra Nevada mountains loomed far in the distance, and Samuel's voice grew fainter each second.

Darn that Samuel. He was always trying to spoil her fun. Sarah knew he wouldn't tell Pa on her, though—he never did. Still, Pa would be coming in from the orchard soon, and Sarah didn't want to get caught.

Reluctantly, Sarah jerked the reins to slow

Rusty down and then pulled them to the left to turn him around. She knew she'd better be getting back. To the right, trees bearing apples, plums, and peaches stretched out like a sea of green. Ahead was the barn and her family's house, its white post fence around it gleaming brightly in the sunlight. Home. Sarah sighed. It would be pretty if it wasn't so awfully boring.

Samuel was waiting at the barn, and Sarah saw that he was frowning. "You're gonna get in big trouble one of these days if Pa catches you riding that horse. You know you're not supposed to. Besides, you're supposed to be giving Princess her bath."

Sarah looked at her brother's dark hair and bright blue eyes. Sometimes it was hard to believe she was Sam's twin. They looked alike, but Sarah thought they couldn't be more different. Samuel was born knowing how to be good, but Sarah found trouble everywhere she turned.

"Sarah, are you listening to me?" Samuel asked.

"Of course I am. You're talking loud enough," Sarah said crossly, dismounting Rusty. Sarah looked toward the side of the barn, where Princess, a fat white pig, was rolling in her muddy pen.

"Why can't you wash Princess?" Sarah asked.

Samuel rolled his eyes. "You know I've been helping Pa with the irrigation ditches since sunup. Besides, washing hogs is woman's work. Pa says so."

Sarah shook her head. "Well, it's not fair. Just like it's not fair that I don't get to ride Rusty and you do," Sarah said, sighing. She lovingly stroked the horse's dark mane, and Rusty turned his neck and looked at her with his big, brown eyes.

Samuel sighed. "I don't see why you always have to go looking for trouble, Sarah. It's so much easier to do what Pa says."

"What kind of trouble?" a voice behind them asked.

Sarah spun around, but she already knew who it was. Pa was standing there, his sunburned arms folded across his chest. With his curly golden hair and dark eyes, he was a handsome man, but his face wore a worried frown.

"There's no trouble, Pa. Sam and I were just teasing each other," Sarah said quickly. She glanced at her brother, who was studying his bare feet. Sam would never lie to Pa, but he didn't like to tattle on Sarah, either. Sarah figured it was because they were twins.

Ben Jefferson shook his head. "I swear, the way you two still tease each other, you'd hardly know you were going to be twelve years old come winter."

"It's all in fun, Pa," Sarah said, but her father didn't seem to hear her. He was eying Rusty.

"Rusty here looks like he's been ridden. It wasn't you, Sarah, was it?" he asked. Sarah nervously fingered her apron strings. Pa turned to Samuel. "What do you know about this, son?"

Samuel opened his mouth to speak, but he was spared from answering by a voice behind their father. "Well, if it isn't Jack and Jill. What are you two up to now?"

"That's just what I'm trying to find out," her father said.

Will Rider took off his hat and ran his hand through his dark hair. Everyone said the twins looked like their mother's younger brother. Ma said that Sarah shared his independent streak, too.

Princess grunted loudly from her pen, and Sarah saw her father's gaze turn to the pig. "Sarah, that pig should have been washed by now. What have you got to say for yourself?"

Sarah avoided her father's angry brown eyes. "I was just about to do it, Pa."

"Well, get to it. It's almost time for supper. Sam, you get those horses groomed and fed."

"Yes, sir," Sam said.

Ben Jefferson turned and walked across the dusty ground toward the house. Uncle Will walked over to Sarah and put his arm on her shoulder.

"Looks like we've got one dirty old sow to clean," Uncle Will said. "I'll help you get the buttermilk from the cellar."

Sarah and her uncle walked to the side of the barn and lifted up the wooden door that led into the small dirt cellar below.

"They don't keep hogs in Los Angeles, do they, Uncle Will?" Sarah asked, struggling to hold up her side of the heavy milk pail. She already knew what the answer would be.

"Not in most parts of the city, no," Uncle Will said. "After all, this is 1905—the beginning of the twentieth century!"

"If you need meat, you can go right to the store and buy it," Sarah said. "That's what I would do. I would never wash a pig, ever, if I lived in the city. I hate getting covered with sticky mud."

"Is that so?" Uncle Will asked, his blue eyes smiling. "You and mud have been friends since you were two."

Sarah laughed. She couldn't fool her uncle. "Well, I just don't understand why we buy a perfectly nice pig in the spring, and take care of it and fatten it up all summer, just so we can kill it." She shuddered.

Uncle Will ruffled her hair. "I don't see you turning down the bacon each morning."

Sarah blushed. "I know, but in the city, I

wouldn't have a chance to be friends with my break-fast."

They were at the pen now, and Princess was snorting happily. Sarah tucked the bottom of her skirt into her waistband and began to pull Princess out of the brown mud. "This is too messy, even for me," she said, wrinkling her nose as Uncle Will tied Princess up outside the pen.

Sarah took a rag, dipped it in the buttermilk, and began to wash the layers of encrusted mud off Princess. "I can't believe you'd rather be out here in the middle of nowhere than back in Los Angeles, Uncle Will. They have everything there. Motor cars. Electric lights." She sighed, and looked out over the rows and rows of trees in the orchard. "All we've got is apples. Millions of apples."

"And plums. And pears. And green fields and open spaces," Will said. He pointed west toward the cloud-capped Sierras. "California's got the most beautiful mountain range in the country and some of the richest soil in the state is right here. We're lucky. Most of Owens Valley is just miles and miles of desert. But we're lucky. The water that runs off the mountains every spring keeps the fields green here in Independence."

Sarah nodded. She had often imagined that the valley would look like a patchwork quilt if you could see it from the sky. Most of the squares would be dry, brown desert, brightened by patches of green where farmers had managed to divert enough water to grow crops.

"But we depend so much on the water we get from the mountains. Ma and Pa are always worried about it," Sarah said. "Sometimes it's hard to keep our irrigation ditches full. What's to keep us from becoming desert again someday?"

"All we need is for the federal government to approve the irrigation project, and we won't have to worry about water anymore," Uncle Will said. "There's enough water in the Owens River for the whole valley. Then this family and everyone else around here won't ever have to want for anything."

"Someday," Sarah muttered. "And even if someday isn't so far off? What happens then? There'll always be trees that need planting, and pigs that need washing. When I'm old enough, I'm going to take Rusty and ride on out of this place." She wiped her dirty hands on her apron, which was just as filthy as the rest of her.

Will shook his head. "I should know better than to try to stop any kin of mine from dreaming," he said. "I rode off to Los Angeles once, but I came back to the country. Had all kinds of big thoughts about the big city. I guess you'll have to make up your own mind, just like I did."

Samuel walked out of the barn. "Sarah, aren't

you finished with that old pig yet? She can't get clean by herself. You'd better hurry or you'll be late for supper." He ran off toward the house.

Sarah sighed. "There goes one more thing I'd like to leave behind someday."

Uncle Will just laughed as he watched Sarah turn dejectedly back to her work.

CHAPTER TWO
They Are Stealing Our Water!

"Sarah Jefferson! Change into some clean clothes before you go anywhere near the supper table," Eliza Jefferson said. Her face was dusted with flour, and her dark hair was coming loose from where she had it pinned up.

"Sorry, Ma," Sarah said. "I was just giving Princess her bath."

Sarah's mother shook her head. "You should have been finished with that an hour ago. I had to get supper ready by myself." Her mother turned to Uncle Will. "You shouldn't have let her get so dirty, Will. Sometimes I think you're still a child yourself."

Uncle Will planted a kiss on his sister's cheek. "Supper sure smells good, Sis."

Her mother's face softened. "Stop trying to

butter me up. And stop staring, Sarah. Go get cleaned up."

"Yes, Ma." Sarah ran up the stairs to her small bedroom. That was one thing she could be thankful for, she thought. Her school friend Becky had to share a room with her brothers and sisters. She couldn't imagine having to share a room with Samuel.

By the time her mother rang the supper bell, Sarah had put on a clean dress and apron and scrubbed her hands and face in the water basin in her room.

Downstairs in the dining room, her father was just sitting down at the head of the table. Four men, the farm's hired hands, were finding their places. In a few weeks, when the fruit was ready for harvesting, Sarah knew there might be as many as ten extra men at the table.

Her father raised an eyebrow as Sarah slid into her seat. "Why are you the last one at the table, Sarah?"

"I was getting cleaned up, Pa. From washing Princess," Sarah said.

"That's right. You were late with your chores today," her father said. "And what was Rusty doing outside the stable this afternoon?"

Sarah's stomach dropped. Her mother's left-over fried chicken and fresh biscuits smelled delicious, but it didn't look as though she was going to enjoy this supper at all.

"Well, Sam took Rusty for a ride. Didn't you, Sam?" Sarah said. Her brother's face turned as red as an apple.

"I see," Pa said, but he fixed his gaze on Sarah. "Well, I'm glad it wasn't you, Sarah. You know how I feel about you riding that horse."

"I know, Pa, but I don't think it's fair—" Sarah began, but a warning glance from her mother stopped her.

Sarah expected her father to be angry, but instead, he looked thoughtful. "I don't think your ma and I have given you enough responsibility in this household, Sarah. You need a worthwhile activity to keep you occupied. Eliza, do you think you have time for a sewing lesson tonight?"

Sewing! Sarah's heart sank. Every time she picked up a needle, it seemed to slip right through her fingers.

Her mother smiled. "I think I have time."

"Good," her father said. He patted Sarah's head. "I'm sure you'll turn into a fine young lady some day."

It's still not fair, Sarah wanted to say, but this time she held her tongue. She was lucky her father hadn't been cross with her.

She felt her mother's arm around her. "Don't

worry, Sarah. We'll patch up that slip of yours tonight. Maybe tomorrow we can go into town with your Uncle Will and pick out some pretty fabric for a new dress. Would you like that?"

"Yes, Ma," Sarah said. Out of the corner of her eye, she could see Samuel grinning.

The early hours of the night were usually Sarah's favorite. The sky would turn from orange, to red, to a deep, thick blue, and finally, so many silvery stars would appear that Sarah couldn't begin to count them. Then the family would sit on the porch and talk, or even sing sometimes. Lately, Uncle Will had been buying the Young Reader's Companion, and Pa would read stories from the magazine. Sarah's favorites were the stories about faraway places, or any story with a horse in it.

But tonight was different. Sarah took her seat next to Pa's chair. He was lighting the coal oil lamp. "No story for you tonight, Sarah," he said, without looking up from the lamp. "You've got that sewing lesson, remember?"

Sarah made a face in the dark. "Yes, Pa," she said. The coal oil lamp sputtered on, and a small cloud of thick black smoke snaked from the top.

"These lamps are ready for a cleaning," Pa said, looking at Sarah. "You'd better take care of that tomorrow."

Sarah sighed. The only thing worse than giving a pig a bath was cleaning a score of oily kerosene lamps. "In Los Angeles, they have electricity. No one has to clean oil lamps there," she muttered softly as she went inside the house. As she walked up the stairs, she heard her father's deep voice as he read to Samuel. Maybe her brother was right to be good all the time. If she had washed Princess when she was supposed to, she would be outside with him right now. Why was it so hard to be good?

"It's going to be another hot one today, Sis," Uncle Will said, looking over his shoulder. He was riding Rusty, who was pulling Sarah and her mother in a small wagon behind him. Sarah didn't need her uncle to tell her how hot it was. It was still morning, but the August sun was already beating down hard.

"You're right about that, Will," Ma said.

Sarah groaned. Her stiff bonnet made her neck itch. To make things worse, a large blister had formed on her finger from her efforts at sewing the night before.

"Do I have to wear this thing?" she whined, pulling at her bonnet strings.

"You'd get sunstroke without it in this heat," her mother said.

"We're not too far now," Uncle Will called

to Sarah's relief. Maybe they'd find some shade in Independence, the town closest to their farm. It was about eight miles away, but the trip usually went fast in the wagon. That suited Sarah just fine. There wasn't much to look at, except a few other farms. This land was greener than most parts of the valley, and other farmers like Pa had planted orchards of fruit trees. Row after row after row of boring trees.

Independence was actually a fairly exciting place, although it couldn't compare to Los Angeles. Usually, she loved taking a trip into town, but Sarah wished they were going for a different reason.

"Ma, can't we just pick a new dress out of the Sears & Roebuck catalog?" Sarah pleaded.

Sarah's mother frowned. "You know we'd have to sell a lot more apples before we could afford store-bought clothes, Sarah."

"That might be sooner than we think, Eliza," Uncle Will said. "If this Reclamation Service project goes through, there will always be plenty of water in the valley. One of the big railroad companies would be sure to come through Independence. When that happens, we'll be able to sell fruit to people all over the country if we want to."

Sarah had heard talk of the Reclamation Service project for the last year. She knew it was a special plan the federal government had to irrigate all of Owens Valley. There was plenty of water in the Owens River, but not all the valley residents had the money or the means to bring the water to their farms. The Reclamation Service project would make sure the farmers who worked the valley had all the water they needed.

"Do you really think it will happen soon?" Sarah asked excitedly. If the railroad came, Independence would become almost as exciting as Los Angeles. All kinds of people would come to the valley to live and open shops and other businesses.

"Things look pretty good," Uncle Will said. He nodded in the direction of the Richardson cattle ranch. "I heard Joe Richardson sold some of his land to Fred Eaton last week. Everyone knows that Eaton represents the Reclamation Service project. If he's got Richardson's land, something must be brewing."

Sarah felt like singing. "That would be wonderful, wouldn't it, Ma?"

Her mother allowed herself a small smile. "Yes, it would. We've all worked hard."

Sarah wished her mother wouldn't be so modest sometimes. Ten years ago, Ma and Pa had come all the way from Boston, Massachusetts, to farm the valley. They only had fifty acres of land, but they'd turned up a good crop every year. They deserved to have something good happen.

As they neared the town, Sarah saw the cluster of wooden buildings that made up the center of Independence. In her excitement, she forgot all about why they had come—to get fabric to make her dress.

"We're here, Ma," she cried happily.

The town was usually quiet, but Sarah saw today that a crowd had gathered in front of the post office. A scowling farmer galloped past the wagon. As the wagon drew closer, Sarah heard an angry buzz rising from the crowd.

"What's going on here?" Uncle Will asked, getting down off Rusty.

James Aguilar, a farmer from outside of town, was holding up a newspaper. "This just came in from Los Angeles."

Sarah started to jump out of the wagon, but her mother held her back. It was easy enough to read the paper's headline, which was written in large letters: "TITANIC PROJECT TO GIVE CITY A RIVER." The paper was dated July 29, 1905, just a few days before.

"What does this mean?" Uncle Will asked, grabbing the paper.

"The Los Angeles water company is planning to build an aqueduct from here to the city," James said. "They are stealing our water!"

Uncle Will looked shocked. "It can't be.

What about the Reclamation Service project?"

"According to this, there is no more Reclamation Service project," the farmer said.

Sarah tugged at her uncle's sleeve. "What's an aqueduct, Uncle Will?" she asked.

"It's a kind of canal that's built to carry water from one place to another," he answered. He walked back to the wagon, his mouth set in a grim line. Sarah was taken aback to see her uncle look so unusually upset.

"I knew something was brewing all right," Uncle Will said, his voice filling of anger. "I just didn't know it was trouble."

CHAPTER THREE
We've Got to Go to This Meeting

"**B**en should hear about this right away," Sarah's mother said, nervously wringing her hands.

"We'll head back to the ranch soon enough," Uncle Will said. "You two take care of your errand. I'll see if I can find out more about what's going on around here."

Sarah jumped out of the wagon. "Ma, can't I go with Uncle Will?"

"I don't want you getting in the way." Her mother's face was firm. "Let's go get that fabric."

Sarah watched longingly as Uncle Will led Rusty to a hitching post near the crowd. She wanted to hear the news for herself.

Still, Sarah brightened a little as she and her mother walked through the door of Ned Tate's general store. Everything a person could want was stuffed into the small store. Sacks of flour and sugar were stacked against one wall. Farming tools hung from hooks on another wall. Delicate watches and brooches rested under a shining glass case, and Sarah's favorite, jars of brightly colored candy, were lined up on a wooden counter.

Ned Tate was standing behind the counter. He peered over his tiny round glasses when they came in. "Why, hello there, Sarah Jefferson," he greeted her, smiling. "Care to tackle one of my riddles today?"

Sarah smiled back. They had been playing this game ever since she could remember. "I'm always ready for that, Mr. Tate," she said.

Mr. Tate's green eyes began to gleam. "All right then. Please tell me: What is more wonderful than a dog that can count?"

Sarah thought for a minute, and the answer seemed to pop into her head. "A spelling bee!"

"Well done, Sarah," Mr. Tate said. "That's a mighty clever girl you have there, Eliza."

Her mother smiled, and Sarah thought she looked a little proud. "Thank you, Ned."

By that time Sarah was in such good spirits that even picking out the fabric turned out to be fun. The bolts of cloth were stacked on a counter in a corner of the store, and Sarah looked through them until she finally settled on a pale blue cotton print with tiny white polka dots. She even talked her mother into buying a length of ribbon to match that she could wear in her hair, just like the girls in the city did.

Sarah had almost forgotten about the news of the aqueduct, until, while he was wrapping their purchases in brown paper, Mr. Tate asked, "So Eliza, will your family be attending the meeting tomorrow night?"

"What meeting? Is it about the aqueduct?" Sarah asked.

Mr. Tate nodded. "It's over at the schoolhouse. Stafford and Mary Austin have called it."

Mary Austin! Last year, their schoolteacher had read part of Mrs. Austin's book *The Land of Little Rain* to the class. It was all about life in Owens Valley.

"Can we go, Ma?" Sarah asked excitedly. She had seen Mary Austin a few times in town, but never up close.

"We'll talk to your pa," her mother said. She took the package from Mr. Tate. "Good day, Ned. And thank you."

"Please, Ma, we've got to go to the meeting. It's important," Sarah said. Her mother was silent. Sarah knew what she was probably thinking. Mary Austin was considered a bit eccentric. She spent most of her time writing her books or visiting the Indian families who lived in the desert.

Outside, Uncle Will was standing by the cart. "Uncle Will, there's an important meeting tomorrow night!" Sarah called out.

"I know," Uncle Will said. "It should clear some things up."

"We'll talk to your pa about this, Sarah," her mother said.

The dusty ride home was silent. Neither Uncle Will nor her mother seemed to want to talk. But Sarah was bursting with excitement. Usually, her pa kept important matters like this from her. He said girls didn't need to know such things. Of course, Samuel said that Pa was right. For once, she knew something that Samuel didn't.

It was still early in the day when they got back to the farm. Uncle Will rode out to the orchard to deliver the news, and Sarah spent the rest of the day doing her chores. The men had brought their lunch out into the orchards, and she wouldn't see her father until supper. If she kept her mind on her chores today, he wouldn't be cross with her. Maybe he'd let her go to the meeting.

"You're quite a busy bee today, Sarah," her mother said approvingly.

"That's me, a busy bee," Sarah sang cheerfully, wiping the sweat from her forehead with the back of her arm. It was bread-baking day, and Sarah was kneading her ma's sticky dough for what seemed like the hundredth time. She had spent nearly two hours in the morning churning butter, and her arms ached. But it was worth it, she thought. Pa would be so pleased.

Finally, the sun was low in the sky, and Ma rang the brass dinner bell. Two jackrabbits sprinted across the dusty ground leading up to the house. Pa and the men emerged from the orchard, looking hot and tired.

When Pa sat down at the table, Sarah couldn't wait any longer. "Did you hear the news, Pa? Did Uncle Will tell you about the meeting?"

Pa looked wearily at his daughter. "Not now, Sarah."

"There's no sense in ignoring it, Ben," Uncle Will said.

Pa's eyes flashed angrily. "I will not talk about this nonsense at the table. It's obvious that someone is spreading rumors."

"I saw it in the newspaper with my own eyes, Ben," Uncle Will said.

Eliza Jefferson put her hand on her husband's shoulder. "I saw it, too, Ben."

Her husband scratched his head. "But it's impossible! No one can build an aqueduct two hundred and thirty-five miles long, and over a mountain range, to boot."

"They said the Panama Canal was impossible, too," Uncle Will said. "But they'll start building that any day now."

Sarah's father sighed. "I suppose we should attend this meeting. We really do need to know about it."

Sarah leapt out of her seat. "Hooray!"

"Not so fast, Sarah," Pa said. "A meeting like this is no place for a young girl."

"But I suppose Samuel can go," Sarah muttered.

"If Samuel goes, that will be my decision," her father said sternly. "Sarah, you are old enough to know how to hold your tongue. Perhaps you should contemplate this in your room."

"Yes, Pa," Sarah said tearfully. She pushed her untouched plate away and ran upstairs.

A few hot tears splashed down Sarah's cheeks as she sat on her bed. It just wasn't fair. Pa let Samuel do anything he wanted.

There was a soft knock on the door, and her mother came in with a ham sandwich and a glass of milk. "Have something to eat, Sarah. Then come help me with the dishes," she said.

Sarah's throat was dry from crying, but, realizing how hungry she was from the day's work, she finished the sandwich before she went downstairs.

Her ma was heating a pot of water on the stove for the dishes. Without saying a word, Sarah filled a second pot of water from the pump outside.

"Your father is right, you know, Sarah," Ma said, when they began the familiar rhythm of washing and rinsing. "You need to learn how to hold your tongue. It'll get you in trouble someday."

"I know, Ma," Sarah said. "It's just that I wanted to go to the meeting so bad."

"So badly," her mother corrected. Then her voice softened. "The meeting's not for another day. Let's see what happens tomorrow."

Sarah brightened. Would her ma actually be on her side? She looked at her mother's face, but couldn't read her expression.

Her father walked into the room, carrying a coal oil lamp and shaking his head. "Sarah, I thought you were going to clean these, child. I don't know what I'm going to do with you."

Sarah felt like crying again. All her hard work today was for nothing. She couldn't seem to do anything right. She looked at her mother. Tomorrow, she thought. Something's got to go right tomorrow.

CHAPTER FOUR
I'll Lose My Farm if That Aqueduct Is Built

"Ben, please try to be reasonable," her mother was saying.

Sarah pressed her ear against the kitchen door. She knew it wasn't right to eavesdrop, but she had to know if she would be allowed to go to the meeting. It was going to start in just an hour.

"There will be other families there," her mother continued. "I spoke to the Hendersons, and they'll all be there, even Becky."

"Well, I'm not sure," Sarah heard her father say.

"I think the meeting could be a good experience for both the children. Mary Austin is a fine author, even if she is a little odd. Hearing her speak could be very educational."

At those words, Sarah smiled. Her mother

had grown up in Boston, where she had gone to fine schools. She was always worried that the twins wouldn't get a proper schooling at their California homestead. In matters of education, her mother's will usually prevailed.

This time was no different. "I suppose you're right," her father said. "I'll hitch up the wagon."

Sarah suppressed a shout and quickly ran away from the door. She sat down on the sofa and picked up her needle and thread, pricking her finger in the process.

Her mother poked her head in the door. "Best get your shoes on, Sarah. We'll be going to the meeting soon. That includes you."

"Thanks, Ma," Sarah said.

Sarah was so excited she nearly tripped climbing into the wagon. Pa and Uncle Will discussed the aqueduct during the ride, and Sarah listened to their every word.

"Los Angeles is a city full of crooks," Uncle Will kept saying. "I'm surprised we didn't see this coming a long time ago."

Sarah was used to hearing comments like this from her uncle. He had lived in Los Angeles for a year, and he never had much good to say about it.

Her father seemed more hopeful than his brother-in-law. "I still can't believe the city would be so dishonest, Will."

"I guess we'll find out tonight," Uncle Will said.

The quiet night got louder as they approached the schoolhouse. Bright lights shone from within. Pa hitched up the wagon, and Sarah and Sam ran ahead into the crowd.

"Behave yourselves!" their mother called after them.

The only room of the tiny schoolhouse was packed with people. Sarah saw her friend Becky Henderson near the front of the room and waved. She'd never be able to get as close as Becky.

"We won't be able to see a thing," Sarah said.

Sam grabbed her arm and pulled her into the crowd. "We might be able to see something from here."

Sarah strained her head and found she was able to see over Sam's shoulder. A woman appeared at the front of the room, and the mumbling died down. She was wearing a brightly colored skirt, a white Mexican blouse, and Shoshone Indian jewelry around her neck.

"That's got to be Mary Austin," Sarah whispered to Sam. No other woman in Independence looked like that, she was sure.

"And that must be her husband, Stafford," Samuel said, pointing to a tall man with glasses standing next to her.

In his dark suit, Stafford Austin looked different from the other ranchers in the room, with their denim dungarees and faded work shirts.

Mary Austin held up her hand. "Thank you all for coming here tonight," she said in a loud, clear voice. The mumbling died out completely. "My husband and I thought it best if all the residents of the valley understood what is happening. I'm sure you've all heard about Los Angeles's plans to build an aqueduct in Owens Valley. Stafford has learned of some information regarding this crisis, which he will explain to you now."

Stafford cleared his throat. "As you know, I hold the position of Registrar of the Land Office in this county," he began. "It came to my attention several weeks ago that Fred Eaton, a former mayor of Los Angeles, was purchasing land along the Owens River. Many of us thought that Eaton was representing the Reclamation Service, and that the land would be used for an irrigation project in Owens Valley. But recently, I began to uncover a sinister scheme.

"It seems that Eaton was not representing the Reclamation Service. Instead, he was buying the land so he could sell it to the Los Angeles Water and Power Company."

"What are you saying?" one of the ranchers called out.

"The water company now owns the riparian rights to the Owens River. Instead of being used for irrigation for our farms and ranches, the water will be sent to Los Angeles," Stafford replied.

A low murmur filled the room. Samuel nudged Sarah. "What are riparian rights?" he whispered.

"Water rights. That means they can use the water any way they choose," she whispered back.

"Isn't there anything we can do?" someone in the crowd asked. Sarah thought she recognized James Aguilar's voice.

"It may be possible to restrict the use of the water," Mary Austin said.

"That's true," Stafford said. "Two weeks ago, I wrote to the Secretary of the Interior. And last week, I wrote to the president himself—Theodore Roosevelt. They both have the power to put limits on how much water Los Angeles can take from us."

Sarah brightened at the mention of President Roosevelt. She had learned about him in school. People called him the "Conservation President" because of his dedication to preserving the wilderness. Surely he would not allow the valley's farms and green fields to dry up.

Now Mary Austin was speaking again. "Remember, too, that the issue must come before the people of Los Angeles in three weeks. They will vote on whether to spend millions of tax dollars on the project. They may refuse to build the aqueduct."

Sarah felt her brother nudge her. "Maybe everything will be all right," he whispered.

Sarah looked at the faces around her. They looked angry and concerned. Uncle Will was scowling grimly.

"People don't look too happy," she whispered back to her brother.

A tall man with a red beard spoke next. It was Becky's father, Merle Henderson. "Mr. Austin, we appreciate you bringing us here. Now we know the whole story. But is writing a couple of letters going to help? It doesn't sound like enough."

"It sure doesn't!" another man shouted. "I have a hard enough time watering my crops as it is. I'll lose my farm if that aqueduct is built."

"We all will," Mary Austin said. "That is why we must raise our voices against this injustice."

"Let's raise our fists instead!" Merle Henderson yelled. "Let's show those city folks we can fight for what's ours!"

The crowd burst into angry shouts and applause, and Sarah felt a little afraid.

Mary Austin spoke again. "We gathered everyone here tonight in hopes that we could present a united front. Many voices are more powerful than one. There is much we can still do. I will be traveling to Los Angeles tomorrow to speak to William Mulholland, head of the water company. I'd like to have your support behind me."

More cheers erupted, and then everyone began talking at once. Some were talking loudly and excitedly to those around them, and others were shouting above the crowd. Suddenly, the room seemed hot and stifling.

Sarah tugged on Samuel's sleeve. "I'm going outside," she said.

"I'm right behind you," her brother replied.

As soon as they stepped outside, Sarah felt better. The loud shouts of the schoolhouse were much weaker out here, and the blanket of stars above her looked peaceful and familiar. Still, she felt confused and worried by what had just happened.

People were filing out of the schoolhouse now. Sarah looked around for her mother and father. She didn't see them, but she spotted Uncle Will leaning against the building. The twins walked up to him.

"Why is everyone so angry, Uncle Will?" Samuel asked.

"I guess they're a little afraid. And they're feeling powerless—like there's nothing they can do," Uncle Will answered.

"But Mr. Austin wrote to the president. Mr. Roosevelt won't let this happen. I know it," Sarah said.

Uncle Will's face softened. "I hope so, Sarah. Listen, why don't you two find your folks? They might be back at the wagon and we should be heading back." Uncle Will took a few steps, then turned back to them. "Don't worry. I'm sure everything will work out."

Samuel headed toward the wagon, but Sarah's eyes followed her uncle. He stepped into a crowd of people who had gathered outside the schoolhouse. They all sounded angry.

Uncle Will approached one of the men and shook his hand. It was dark, and Sarah couldn't be sure, but it looked like Merle Henderson.

"Come on, Sarah," Samuel said as he started toward their wagon.

Sarah turned to follow her brother. She didn't like the looks of things. It felt like trouble. What were the people planning to do? She knew they were angry, but they wouldn't do something foolish just because they were angry, would they?

Sarah wasn't sure, but she had a funny feeling in the pit of her stomach.

CHAPTER FIVE
Sarah's Plan

"**W**ake up, Sarah. We're home." The wagon carrying the family creaked to a stop.

Sarah opened her eyes to see her mother leaning over her. She must have fallen asleep on the ride home from the meeting.

"Up to bed, now," her mother said.

Sarah climbed out of the wagon clumsily. The night was pitch black now, and the sound of chirping crickets was the only noise she heard. The buzzing sound of the angry crowd was only a faint echo in her mind.

Samuel was barely awake, and Pa and Uncle Will looked tired and worried.

"The president will take care of everything, Pa," Sarah said sleepily.

Her father kissed her on the forehead, and

Sarah started up the stairs. Once in her room, Sarah put on her cotton nightgown and began to brush out her long hair. The window was open, but there was no breeze.

Sarah sprawled out on top of her quilt. "I'll never get to sleep in this heat," she muttered.

Just then, the sound of voices drifted up from the porch below. One of the voices sounded angry. It was Uncle Will. Sarah walked to the window.

"I can't believe you're just going to sit back and take this, Ben," Uncle Will said. "You and Eliza have worked so hard all these years."

"We're not sitting back, Will." Sarah recognized her mother's voice. "But we've got to exhaust all the possibilities before we give in to our anger. I think Mary Austin's plans were promising."

Her father spoke. "I hate to see you get riled up for no good reason, Will. You're too hot-headed sometimes. You've got to be a little patient."

"There's no harm in talking to Merle Henderson tomorrow," Uncle Will said. "We should at least hear what else he has to say."

"I just don't like it. Merle has been known to turn to violence before. He nearly shot the man who sold him those sick cattle," her mother said. "I think we should wait and hear what the president has to say."

"You sound just like Sarah, Eliza. Teddy

Roosevelt has got other things to worry about besides Owens Valley," her father said. "Maybe you're right, Will. I suppose there's no harm in talking to Merle. I'll go with you."

Sarah heard the creak of the front door opening and walked back to her bed. Her mother's warning of violence stuck in her mind. She had heard how angry the ranchers were tonight, especially Merle Henderson. Would Pa and Uncle Will get mixed up in the trouble somehow?

She still couldn't fall asleep. It was more than the heat that was keeping her awake. Life on the farm was sometimes tiresome, but the thought of losing everything they had worked so hard for was scary.

There must be some solution to this, Sarah thought, staring out at the night sky. She thought about what Stafford and Mary Austin had said. They were taking action by talking to people and asking for help. Stafford had even written to the president. That makes a lot of sense, Sarah thought, even though Pa thinks it's foolish.

Thoughts darted in and out of Sarah's mind like fireflies. Before she finally drifted off to sleep, she thought she knew what to do.

"Milking's all done, Ma," Sarah said. She had gotten up extra early this morning. She had a plan.

"Sarah, you've been working so hard lately," her mother said approvingly. She was spooning oatmeal into bowls for breakfast. "I'll sure miss having you around when school starts again."

"I was thinking about that today, Ma," Sarah said. "Do you think I could use your paper and ink? I want to practice my penmanship before school begins."

"Why, how industrious," her mother said. Sarah could tell she was pleased. "Of course you may. You've certainly caught up on your chores."

"Thank you, Ma," Sarah said. She was happier than her ma knew. The first part of her plan was going smoothly.

After breakfast, Sarah rushed through the dishes and ran to her mother's writing desk in the parlor. She took a bottle of ink, a pen, a piece of parchment paper, and an envelope from the top drawer. Her mother always had writing supplies on hand so she could write to her cousins in Boston.

Sarah opened the bottle of ink, careful not to spill a drop. She dipped the pen into the ink, and began her letter: "Dear Mr. President."

Sarah had figured last night that if enough people told the president about what was happening in the valley, he would have to listen.

Sarah bit the end of her pen. She wasn't sure what Stafford Austin had written in his letter. What was she supposed to say?

There was an open window in front of the desk, and Sarah looked out at her family's farm. A red-tailed hawk flew over the neat rows of fruit trees. The small stretch of rocky land between the house and the orchard was dotted with wild almond bushes and lupines that bloomed brilliant colors in the spring and early summer.

Just outside the valley, Sarah knew, the land was not so green. It was dry, dusty desert. Uncle Will had always said that Owens Valley was a slice of paradise in California. For the first time, she understood what her uncle meant.

Sarah picked up the pen. "I am eleven years old. I have lived in Owens Valley almost all my life," she wrote. "The land here is green and beautiful. Many farmers grow hay and fruit and wheat. Without the water from the Owens River, all our fields would dry up."

As she wrote, Sarah began to wonder why the people in Los Angeles thought they could take their water. She even began to feel a little bit of Uncle Will's anger.

"The people in the city think they need the water more than we do. But aren't we just as important? After all, we grow food for people to eat.

"Please help us. Please do not let them build the aqueduct. Thank you."

There, that sounded right, Sarah thought. She added a closing and signed her name. When the ink was dry, she folded the letter, slipped it into the envelope, and shoved it in her pocket.

Now, all she had to do was get into town. She knew her mother was pleased that all her chores were done. The second part of her plan was to get Ma to let her go to the creek for a few hours.

CHAPTER SIX
Get Off That Horse Right Now!

"**W**hat a wonderful idea," her mother said a short while later. "While you're there, you can pick some blackberries. It's been a while since I made a blackberry pie."

"Sure, Ma. I'll head out now," Sarah said. She grabbed two biscuits off the table. "I'll have these and some berries for lunch."

"Don't be too long," Ma said, handing her a basket.

Sarah ran out of the house, her heart pounding. She felt in her pocket to make sure the letter was still safely tucked away. Then she headed toward the barn.

She knew Pa wouldn't have taken Rusty out today. He and all the men, including Samuel, were out in the orchard irrigating the trees. Ma couldn't see the barn from the kitchen. Sarah knew if she hurried, she could ride into town, post the letter, and even pick the berries before it got too late. And no one in her family would know about it until they heard from the president himself.

"Hello, Rusty," Sarah said, as she saddled the horse. "I missed you."

A few minutes later, she was galloping toward Independence, keeping a sharp eye out for any gopher holes that might trip up the horse. Rusty seemed to fly beneath her, and they arrived in no time at all.

The postmaster raised an eyebrow when Sarah asked for the address of the president, but Sarah told him it was a summer assignment for school. She was even able to pay for the postage with the nickel that Ma's cousin Rose had sent her for her birthday.

Sarah was mounting Rusty when she heard a voice behind her.

"You're in town all by yourself today, eh Sarah?" It was Mr. Tate.

"I'm just running an errand." Her heart was beating nervously.

"Can you tell me, Sarah, what the difference is between a watchmaker and a jailer?" Mr. Tate asked.

Sarah relaxed. He didn't seem to think it was

unusual for her to be riding Rusty. Still, she was too nervous to try to answer his riddle. "I give up," she said, shrugging.

Mr. Tate grinned widely. "One sells watches, and the other watches cells."

Sarah laughed weakly, and picked up Rusty's reins.

"Good-bye, Mr. Tate!" she called as she rode away. Then she leaned down and whispered in the horse's ear, "That was a close one, Rusty."

Sarah was careful not to ride past the house on the way back to the barn. As she crossed the field next to the orchard, her heart pounded with excitement. She had done it! The president would read her letter and stop the trouble brewing in the valley.

"Sarah Jefferson! What do you think you're doing?"

Sarah pulled hard on Rusty's reins. It was Pa. She had been so lost in thought that she hadn't seen him.

"Get off that horse right now!" Ben Jefferson yelled.

Sarah's hands shook as she climbed out of the saddle. "I can explain, Pa," she said.

"Well, I'd sure like to hear an explanation. You know you are not allowed to ride that horse. What's gotten into you?" her father asked.

"I went —" Sarah began, then stopped. If Pa knew she had gone all the way into town, she'd be in worse trouble than she was now. "Ma wanted me to pick some berries by the creek. I thought it would be faster if I took Rusty," she lied.

Her father eyed the empty basket hanging from Rusty's saddle. "What happened to the berries?"

Sarah thought quickly. "I dropped them when Rusty started to go real fast."

Her father shook his head. "That is exactly why I don't want you riding that horse. Lord knows what could happen to a young girl like you out riding by herself," he said.

"But I'm a good rider!" Sarah said, without thinking. "Nothing's going to happen to me."

As soon as the words slipped out, Sarah knew she had said too much. The color was rising to her father's face.

"That will be enough, Sarah," he said angrily.

"Now, I want you to walk back to the creek and get those berries for your ma like you should have done before. Then you can be sure your ma and I will see to it that you're too busy from now on to be riding that horse ever again."

"Yes, Pa," Sarah said, trying to keep from crying. Only little girls cried. She grabbed the basket and ran off toward the stream.

It was past noon when Sarah returned to the house, her basket filled with berries. Sarah had dreaded going back to the house at all. Riding off on Rusty had been one thing. It was exciting, almost like an adventure. But she had never told such a big lie before. It left a sick feeling in her stomach.

Her mother was outside the house beating some rugs clean with a stick.

"Where's Pa?" Sarah asked, afraid that he was inside.

Her mother put down the stick and took the berries from Sarah. "I packed him some food to take to the orchard. Why don't you and I have some lunch now?"

The cold chicken Ma set before her looked delicious, but she just didn't feel like eating it. She picked at the food on her plate with a fork.

"Sarah, your father told me you were riding Rusty this morning. Do you want to tell me what this is all about?" her mother asked. Her expression was serious, but not angry.

Sarah had hated lying to her father. She couldn't bear having to do it again. "I lied to him, Ma," Sarah said. Tears welled in her eyes. "I rode Rusty into town today because I wrote a letter to the president, and I had to post it. I had to tell him how important it was to save the valley."

Her mother gasped. "Sarah, you rode all the way into town? Why didn't you tell us? We would have posted the letter for you."

"I wanted it to be a surprise. I thought if I told you about it, you wouldn't believe that I could really help. I know Pa wouldn't think so," Sarah said.

"Sarah, it was very dangerous for you to do what you did," her mother said. She sighed, then put a hand on Sarah's shoulder. "I don't approve of it, but I understand it."

"You do?"

Her mother nodded. "Your father is a good man, Sarah, and he's got some very strong opinions about the way the world should be. Now, I don't always agree with those opinions, but the way to change your father's mind is not by acting foolish."

"You mean like riding off by myself?" Sarah asked.

"Exactly. I'll tell you what we'll do. Your father wants you to stay close to the house for a while. I think that's a good idea. We can work on your new dress. When the time is right, we'll see if you can ride Rusty again. But not by yourself."

Sarah threw her arms around her mother. "Thank you, Ma. I'm so sorry."

Her mother looked into Sarah's face. "I have to say I'm surprised you wrote that letter, Sarah. I thought you didn't like living in the valley. I don't see why a person would go to so much trouble to save something they didn't want."

"I guess it's not so bad here," Sarah said, and she meant it. "Besides, what's happening with the aqueduct isn't right. And when something's not right, you have to change it, don't you?"

"I'm proud of you," her mother said quietly. "I won't tell your Pa about the letter just yet. Let's wait and see what happens."

CHAPTER SEVEN
There's Too Much at Stake Here to Sit Still

The days that followed seemed to be the longest days in Sarah's life. It was bad enough not riding Rusty, but she couldn't even go near the barn. And her eyes were strained from sewing those tiny little stitches in her new dress every night.

To make matters worse, it was the end of the summer and the weather was hotter than Sarah ever remembered. Every day it was over 100 degrees. And the hot weather made Pa even more anxious about the aqueduct.

Sarah noticed that Pa and Uncle Will hadn't spoken to each other much since the meeting at Merle Henderson's house, except to argue. As the day of the vote to fund the aqueduct grew nearer, things at the farm seemed more and more tense.

Finally, the heat wave broke. Sarah sat with

Samuel and her mother and father on the porch one night in early September, enjoying a soft breeze. An owl's hoot broke the stillness every few minutes.

"What a beautiful night," her mother said, looking out at the stars.

"It sure is," her father agreed. He seemed to be in a good mood, Sarah thought. "You know, tonight's a good night for a story. Samuel, fetch the Young Reader's Companion."

"Yes, Pa," Sam said eagerly.

Sarah sighed. "I guess I'll get my sewing."

"No need for that tonight," her father said. "You've been working very hard lately, Sarah, and I'm proud of you."

From the corner of her eye, Sarah saw her mother slip her a small smile.

But the peaceful night was shattered as the sound of hoofbeats reached them. Looking out into the night, Sarah saw that it was her uncle.

Uncle Will pulled his horse, Midnight, to a halt and jumped to the ground. He was out of breath. "It's just what we thought, Ben. News of the Los Angeles vote on the aqueduct came through. The bond issue passed. Now the water company has the money they need to take away our water. They'll start building the aqueduct any day now."

"Blast it!" said her father, rising in his chair.

Uncle Will stepped onto the porch. "Merle

Henderson was right all along, Ben. Talking doesn't do any good. We need to send a message that Los Angeles will be sure to hear."

"What kind of message?" Samuel asked.

"He means a violent one," Ma said abruptly. "Will, I wish you wouldn't keep talking to that man. Violence never solved anything."

Uncle Will slammed his fist into the porch railing. "Eliza, it's about time you woke up and saw what is happening. There is too much at stake here to sit still. I'll do whatever it takes to save this valley, and if that means violence, then so be it." He stepped down from the porch. "You just think about it, Ben. I think you know what needs to be done."

Sarah watched as Uncle Will got back up on Midnight and rode off into the night. She was shocked. She had never seen him so angry.

"Don't worry about your uncle," Ma said. "He'll cool down with time."

Sarah looked at her father. "Pa, you don't think Uncle Will is right, do you? Is violence the only thing that will save the valley?"

Her father didn't answer. He stared out into the night, and his face looked more troubled than Sarah had ever seen it.

"Don't do this, Ben. It's foolish," Sarah's mother pleaded.

• • • • •

Sarah was crouched at the top of the darkened stairway. Her mother and father had been arguing ever since Uncle Will had delivered the news about the vote in Los Angeles the night before. Now they were in the kitchen, and Sarah was sure something was about to happen.

"Eliza, I'm not going along to cause trouble. I might be able to help keep things under control," her father said.

"Ben, I don't see the sense in harming Joe Richardson. He hasn't done anything wrong."

Sarah held back a gasp. Could the men really be planning such a thing?

"Now, Eliza, nobody's going to harm Joe," her father said. "But you can't say he's done nothing wrong. He's sold most of his land to Fred Eaton, and he's about to sell the rest. Joe may as well be in league with the devil. We've got reason to be angry with him."

"And what if you can't keep things under control?" her mother asked sharply.

A door slammed, and Sarah heard loud footsteps. It was her uncle.

"The others will be here soon, Ben. Are you coming?" he asked.

Her father looked at her mother, then back at Uncle Will. "I'll be right there."

Uncle Will turned around and left the house without saying another word.

Ma's voice was cold. "You have two children who depend on you, Ben. I hope you remember them tonight."

"Maybe that's why I have to do this," Pa answered softly.

Sarah watched as he grabbed his hat and walked toward the door. She felt a tap on her shoulder, and jumped. But it was only Samuel.

"Sarah, what's going on? Something's happening outside by the barn," he said.

"Let's get away from the stairs," Sarah whispered, her voice barely a hiss.

The twins crept into Sam's room.

"See? Look down there," Samuel said.

Sarah moved next to him. It was dark, but the moon lit up the scene below. Her father and Uncle Will headed toward the barn where other men on horseback were waiting for them. Some of the men were carrying oil lamps that glowed orange in the dark night.

Outside, a loud voice broke the silence. "Are we ready to stand up for ourselves?" Sarah recognized that voice. It was Merle Henderson.

The men all cheered in response, but it was an angry cheer, and the sound made Sarah even more afraid. Sadly, she watched the men ride off.

The night should have been silent once again, but Sarah thought she heard something strange. "Sam, do you hear a crackling noise?" She looked at the barn. She saw the bright orange glow again, but this time it wasn't an oil lamp.

"It's the barn," she said, her voice rising to a scream. "The barn—it's on fire!"

CHAPTER EIGHT
We've Got to Get Doc Willis Out Here

"**G**ood lord!" her mother cried as Sarah ran past her toward the barn. Sarah's bare feet pounded the hard ground, and she could hear her mother and brother behind her.

The flames were climbing up the back wall of the barn. Through the crackling of the fire, Sarah heard a chorus of frightened cries.

"The animals! We've got to get them out!" she yelled.

A thick wave of heat hit her as soon as she got near the blaze. The strong smell of smoke made Sarah take a step back.

Ma grabbed her shoulder. "Sarah, come away. It's too dangerous."

"But Ma, Rusty's in there. And two other horses —and the cows." She struggled out of her mother's grasp and pulled at the heavy barn door. It felt hot to her touch.

"We can do it, Sarah!" Samuel was at her side. With a great heave, they pulled the barn door open. The sharp smell of smoke filled her nose, and Sarah covered her face with her hand.

"We can save them! The fire hasn't reached the stalls yet!" Samuel said. He ran to where the family's two dairy cows were tied up and began working frantically at the ropes.

Sarah strained to see through the smoke. The sound of the fire was louder now, but she was too worried about the animals to be frightened. Now the smoke was making her cough. She ripped off the corner of her nightgown and tied it around her face.

Where was Rusty? Sarah coughed again. It was getting harder to breathe. Rusty's stall was on the left. But which one was it? It was so hard to see. Finally, Sarah found Rusty's stall. The horse was tossing his head wildly in terror. Sarah reached in and grabbed the leather bridle, then opened the gate.

"Just follow me, Rusty," Sarah said. She prayed the horse would let her lead him to safety.

It seemed like the flames were getting closer as Sarah raced out of the barn, keeping a tight hold on Rusty. The horse all but pulled her along to safety.When they were outside, Sarah gasped hard for breath.

"Sarah, Samuel, we've done enough. It's too dangerous," their mother called over the sound of the flames. Her face was covered with black soot, and Sarah could see that she had led the last cow out of the barn.

"But Jake is still in there!" Samuel said. "I've got to get him!"

"Samuel, no!" their mother cried out, but he didn't hear her.

Sarah watched the barn in alarm. The fire was raging now, and the flames were rising high off of the roof. Ma was right. It was too dangerous for Samuel to be there, even if it was to save their last horse.

Suddenly, a loud, splintering sound filled the air. Sarah looked up in horror to see a section of the barn's roof cave in.

"Samuel!" she screamed, and rushed back toward the barn.

Jake emerged from the flames at a fast gallop. But where was her brother? Ma ran past her back into the barn, and Sarah pulled the cloth over her face again and followed.

Samuel was lying face down just a few feet inside the barn. A piece of wood covered his left leg. It must have trapped him in that way when the roof collapsed during the fire.

Her mother strained to lift the wood. With a groan, she managed to pull it off Sam's leg and heave it to the side. Sarah grabbed her brother's shoulders, and together, they carried him out of the barn.

When they were a safe distance from the fire, they lowered him to the ground. Samuel's eyes were closed, and Sarah was suddenly afraid. "Is he all right?" she asked.

"We need help," her mother said firmly. "Sarah, I know you can ride Rusty, but do you think you can ride him bareback? We've got to get Doc Willis out here."

Sarah was stunned. *Could* she do it? She had ridden to Independence only once before, and that was in daylight. But Samuel looked so still. He needed her help.

"I can do it, Ma," Sarah said.

Her mother hugged her. "I love you, Sarah," she said. Sarah could feel her mother's wet tears on her cheek.

"I love you, too, Ma," Sarah said.

With a boost from her mother, Sarah mounted Rusty. The horse was still jittery from the fire.

Sarah grabbed onto Rusty's mane. "It's all right, Rusty," she said. "You're safe now. Now we've got to help Samuel. Giddyap!" She kicked her heels as hard as she could into the horse's flanks.

The sound of the fire was behind her as Sarah rode off into the night. She clung tightly to Rusty's mane. All she could think of was Samuel's still, white face. She had to get to Independence before it was too late.

CHAPTER NINE
We've Decided to Stay in the Valley

"Good boy, Rusty," Sarah called softly. The horse was keeping a steady pace, but Sarah was uneasy. The road was so dark, and her eyes were still stinging from the smoke in the barn. She was beginning to wonder if she was headed in the right direction.

"We can't let Samuel down," Sarah said aloud. Suddenly, she heard voices up ahead. With relief she saw her father and the men. They must have had to make another stop on the way to the Richardson ranch.

Sarah dug into Rusty's flanks. "Pa! Help!"

"What in blazes—" her father began.

Sarah tried to catch her breath. "The barn's on fire, Pa. We got the animals out, but Samuel's hurt bad. I'm going to get Doc Willis in

Independence."

"I'll go on with Sarah. The rest of you will need to get to the barn," Uncle Will said urgently.

"Let's go!" her father yelled, and the men turned around and followed.

"Come on now, Sarah," Uncle Will said, and he headed on toward town.

Sarah's legs ached from riding bareback, but she managed to keep pace with Uncle Will. It wasn't easy finding Doc Willis's house in the dark, and they had to bang loudly on the door before the doctor woke up. When he found out Samuel was hurt, though, he quickly dressed and grabbed his black bag. Soon they were racing out of Independence.

When they finally neared the farm, the barn was a terrifying sight to see. It was engulfed in flames now, and some of the men were carrying water buckets in from the orchard, while others tried to keep the cows and horses from running. But where were her mother and father and Samuel?

Leaping off Rusty, Sarah ran toward the house. She could hear Doc Willis and Uncle Will right behind her.

Sarah ran up the stairs to Samuel's room. Her brother lay on the bed, his eyes still closed. His mother had covered him with blankets.

"I carried him in. He's breathing fine, but I

think his leg's broken," she said.

Doc Willis leaned over the bed. "Give me just a minute with the boy."

In the hallway, Sarah threw her arms around her mother. "Will he be okay?"

Her mother smiled weakly. "I think so, now that help's here."

Her father walked up the stairs. His hands and face were black with soot.

"How's the boy?" Pa asked. His voice was breaking, and Sarah could see that he was holding back tears.

"I think he'll be fine, thanks to his sister. Sarah did a very brave thing tonight," his wife said.

Mr. Jefferson looked at his daughter. "Yes, I guess she did."

"What about the barn, Pa?" Sarah asked, although she knew what the answer would be.

Her father shook his head. "It looks like a spark from one of our lanterns may have started it. It's too far gone to save now. Not that we could have done much good anyway. There isn't enough water in the irrigation ditches to put out a blaze like this," he said sadly.

His wife hugged him. "Our family is safe," she said. "That's what's important."

"Ma, when was George Washington elected

president?" Sarah asked. A week had passed since the fire, and a lot had happened. Pa and the hired hands were working on rebuilding the barn. For Sarah, school had started once again. Her sewing lessons had finally stopped, but she had replaced them with homework.

Of course, that was not Samuel's worry yet. Her brother would probably have to stay in bed for a couple of weeks until his leg mended. But Ma was showering him with attention, and he didn't seem to mind.

So now Sarah was stuck doing homework, and everything was back to the way it was before. Nobody seemed to remember that she had ridden Rusty and saved Samuel. Her father still wouldn't let her ride the horse at all. It just wasn't fair.

"Sarah, I expect you'll find the answer to your question somewhere in your schoolbook," her mother said, shaking her head. She stepped to the door and rang the bell. "Supper!" she called.

Her father walked into the kitchen and patted Sarah's head. "My, Sarah, that new dress of yours looks fine. Aren't you glad you learned how to sew?"

"Yes, Pa." Sarah sighed and looked down at her blue dress. It was pretty, she had to admit. But she would much rather be riding a horse than sewing a dress any day. Why couldn't Pa see that?

"That's my girl," her father said. "I'll go carry Samuel in for supper."

Uncle Will rode up on Midnight and hitched her outside the house. He was carrying a sack of mail over his shoulder.

"We've got some letters today," Uncle Will announced as he walked in.

"From the family in Boston?" her mother asked.

"There's one from Boston," he said. "And, let's see—there's one for Sarah, too. From Washington, D.C. I wonder who it could be from?" There was a twinkle in his eye.

Sarah couldn't believe what she was hearing. "From Washington, D.C.?" she echoed. It couldn't be. "It's from the president!" she cried excitedly.

Mr. Jefferson carried Samuel into the room and set him down on a chair. "The president? What's this all about, Sarah?"

"Open it, Sarah," Samuel urged.

Sarah carefully tore at the letter's seal. This was the day she had been waiting for.

Even her mother was excited. "What's it say?" she asked.

Sarah read the letter. "He says thank you for showing concern about the aqueduct. But he thinks it's important to bring water to a growing city. After all, he says, there are now 250,000 people in Los

Angeles. He also says Los Angeles has suffered through a drought for ten years and they desperately need water. The city could be important to the future of our country." Her voice was filled with disappointment. "But then it says that he approves of using the water for domestic use only. What does that mean?"

Her father was reading the letter over her shoulder. "That means he thinks the water from the aqueduct should be used only in people's homes, not for businesses or farms. That would take too much water away from us." Her father stroked his chin. "That sounds like a fair solution, if the people of Los Angeles listen."

Uncle Will nodded his head, and the men in the kitchen murmured in agreement.

"There's just one thing I'd like to know, Sarah," her father said. "When exactly did you write a letter to the president?"

Sarah looked at her mother. Ma nodded her head.

"Well, it's kind of a long story, Pa," Sarah said weakly. She explained why she wrote the letter, and how she had ridden Rusty into Independence to post it.

"Gosh, Sarah." Her brother's eyes were wide.

Her father looked thoughtful. "To be honest, Sarah, I don't know whether to be angry or proud."

Her mother spoke up. "Maybe we could give proud a try, Ben. Sarah was brave during the fire. And her letter to the president was a smart idea."

"I guess I am proud," her father said. "You know, your ma and I have made some decisions this week, and I'd like to make one more."

"What kind of decisions?" Sarah asked.

"Well, we've decided to stay in the valley, even with the aqueduct coming. This is our land, and we've got to fight for it, but—" he said.

Uncle Will looked at the ground. "I'm ashamed that we thought about roughing up Joe Richardson. Nothing good ever comes from violence. I'll always feel responsible for what happened to Sam's leg."

"I'm just as responsible as you, Will," Sarah's father said, putting a hand on Uncle Will's shoulder. "We can learn from our mistakes. There's been talk of holding another meeting to see if we can come up with some solutions of our own. Maybe we can reach some kind of a compromise. They say the government may build a reservoir for the valley farms when they build the aqueduct. That way, we'd still get water."

"That's wonderful, Pa," Sarah said. "I don't think we should leave, either."

"Hooray!" Samuel yelled.

"Of course, there's one more thing," her

father said. "I think you should be able to ride Rusty every once in a while, if you like."

Sarah flung her arms around her father. "Oh, Pa!" she said. "Can I ride him out in the field?"

"If you like," Pa said.

She sat down at the table, and Uncle Will leaned toward her, a wide grin on his face.

"You know, Sarah, if you run off to Los Angeles, you won't be able to ride Rusty on a wide open field," he whispered.

Sarah grinned back. "Maybe I've changed my mind about running away to Los Angeles. I guess it's not so bad here."

"I always said this place was a slice of paradise," Uncle Will said. Then Sarah heard him say softly, almost to himself, "I just hope it stays that way."

Courtesy of The Los Angeles Times

TITANIC PROJECT TO GIVE CITY A RIVER.

Thirty Thousand Inches of Water to be Brought to Los Angeles.

Options Secured on Forty Miles of River Frontage in Inyo County—Magnificent Stream to be Conveyed Down to the Southland in Conduit Two Hundred and Forty Miles Long—Stupendous Deal Closed.

A 1905 Los Angeles newspaper announced the start of the aqueduct project with great excitement.

Most of the characters in the story are made up, including Sarah Jefferson and her family. However, Los Angeles did announce plans, in the summer of 1905, to build an aqueduct from the Owens Valley to the city. Many farming families were worried about what would happen if they lost their water supply. When the plans for

Mary Altier

*The Owens Lake and nearby valley, shown in a recent
photo, provided an oasis in the California desert.*

the real aqueduct were first made public, the residents of Owens Valley were angry and afraid, but unlike the people in this story, they didn't resort to violence—at least not in the beginning. In fact, life in the valley was peaceful for the next twelve years or so.

Initially, the City of Los Angeles took water only from the lower end of the valley, first making sure that the needs of the valley's residents were met. In addition, a railroad connection finally came to the valley, linking the area to the rest of the country and enabling the farmers and ranchers to become prosperous by selling their goods in other markets.

But in the early 1920s, things changed. A drought struck Southern California, and the

William Mulholland, shown here, Joseph Lippincott, and Fred Eaton were known as the three fathers of the aqueduct.

Courtesy of the Los Angeles Dept. of Water and Power

water supply was depleted. At the same time, Los Angeles was booming, and its thirst was increasing along with its population. More than 100,000 people were moving to the city each year. To satisfy all these newcomers, the city took water from higher and higher up the Owens Valley.

Without enough water to irrigate their land, many farmers and ranchers sold what they owned—along with their water rights—to Los Angeles for a good price. Then they began to move out of the valley. In 1924, some Owens Valley residents, angry because Los Angeles wouldn't buy out their land as well, dynamited the aqueduct in several places. When Los Angeles still did not offer to purchase the land, Owens Valley farmers and townspeople shut off one of the aqueduct gates and diverted water back to the Owens River. More than a thousand people joined the protest and camped out by the gate they had seized. They stayed for four days, leaving only when representatives of Los Angeles agreed to buy the remaining Owens Valley water rights. By the following year, Los Angeles owned all the water rights in the district.

Courtesy of the Los Angeles Dept. of Water and Power

At a celebration on November 5, 1913, water from the Owens River was released into the San Fernando Valley.

MORE ABOUT...

Although most of the characters in Fire in the Valley are fictional, four are not: Fred Eaton, Stafford Austin, Mary Austin, and, of course, President Theodore Roosevelt.

Fred Eaton, a former city engineer and mayor of Los Angeles, was one of the originators of the proposal to build the aqueduct. Eaton wanted to supply Los Angeles with water and make money in the process. He bought land in Owens Valley, saying that his purchases were for the Reclamation Service irrigation project, but then he sold the property to Los Angeles at a huge profit. Eaton knew all along that the land would be used to build the aqueduct.

Stafford Austin was the registrar of the United States Land Office in Owens Valley and used his position to speak out against the aqueduct. However, the meeting he and Mary Austin hold in the story isn't based on any events that really happened.

Mary Austin was a writer who became popular during her career for her style of describing the world around her. A lifelong naturalist, Austin spent many years in

Owens Valley, studying the plants, animals, and people there. Her most famous book, *A Land of Little Rain*, explores life in Owens Valley at the turn of the century. In 1917, Austin wrote a novel, *The Ford*, about the Owens Valley water crisis. Before her death in 1934, she produced 32 books, as well as plays, poems, and essays.

Theodore Roosevelt was the twenty-sixth president of the United States (1901-1909). Roosevelt favored building the Los Angeles aqueduct. He felt that diverting water from Owens Valley to the growing city would serve a greater number of American citizens.

California and Water

The story of the Owens Valley struggle isn't the only time that Californians have argued over water rights. The state's most best-known fight over water use began in 1901, when the mayor of San Francisco proposed damming a river in the Hetch Hetchy Valley.

Mayor James D. Phelan said the dam would bring drinking water and electricity to San Francisco, then a rapidly growing city. But John Muir, a famous conservationist, said that building the dam would destroy what he and a significant group of his friends considered to be one of the most beautiful places on Earth.

Soon, the whole country was embroiled in the debate, which lasted for 12 years. In 1913, the U.S. Senate passed a bill that allowed the dam to be constructed.

Muir may have lost his battle to save the Hetch Hetchy Valley, but naturalists never forgot what he had done in the cause of conservation. Since then, many areas have been exempted from development through the efforts of people like John Muir.

Books in the *Stories of the States* series:

American Dreams
Drums at Saratoga
by Lisa Banim

Children of Flight Pedro Pan
by Maria Armengol Acierno

Fire in the Valley
Mr. Peale's Bones
Voyage of the Half Moon
by Tracey West

East Side Story
Golden Quest
by Bonnie Bader

Forbidden Friendship
by Judith Eichler Weber

Message for General Washington
by Vivian Schurfranz